The Twelve Days of Christmas in Texas

written and illustrated by
Janie Bynum

STERLING

New York / London

¡Holá, Ashley!

Are you ready to see Texas? I think you'll like the warm, sunny days we're having this winter.

I can't wait to celebrate the twelve days of Christmas with you! Since Mom and Dad will be staying home with the new baby, Walita and Lito planned quite an adventure for us. We'll be taking a road trip all over this huge state! Did you know that Texas is larger than New England, New York, Pennsylvania, Ohio, and Illinois combined? Lito says he and Walita will take turns at the wheel—even driving all night—so we can cover as much highway as possible. (We have the best grandparents ever!)

Walita wants to rent a cabaña on the Gulf of Mexico. I love the beach in the wintertime because I don't have to share the shells with the summer tourists. You know how I love seashells!

¡Feliz navidad!

Your cousin, José

2403
OUTLOOK

START

Howdy y'all!

Flying for the first time was amazing! Lito and José picked me up at the Dallas–Fort Worth Airport while Walita prepared a Texas-sized feast for us. We ate barbecue, corn-on-the-cob, and homemade pecan pie!

The nuts came from their pecan tree out back. Lito told us how he used to have to fight the squirrels for the nuts! But this past November, instead of waiting for the pecans to fall to the ground, he tapped the limbs with a padded stick while José and Walita gathered the ones that fell. Looks like Lito is going to be eating lots of pecan pie this year!

As we sat on the porch, I heard a bird singing a bunch of different songs instead of just one. High up in the limbs of the big pecan tree, a pretty gray-and-white mockingbird was singing all those songs. Walita said that <u>Señor Boca</u> must have come out to welcome me to Texas since mockingbirds don't normally sing much in the winter months. José told me that mockingbirds can even mock the sounds of barking dogs and ringing telephones! Now THAT's something I'd like to hear!

Hugs & kisses,
Ashley

P.S. I've really missed Walita's cooking!

nut from shell

shell from pod

On the first day of Christmas,
my cousin gave to me . . .

a mockingbird
in a nut tree.

Dear Mom and Dad,

You wouldn't believe how many pictures Walita has painted since Lito built her a studio! The walls are covered with beautiful fields of bluebonnets and swarms of monarch butterflies. (Walita is fascinated by the state flower and the state butterfly.)

I wish I could see a field of real bluebonnets, but they only bloom from mid-March through May. Walita's paintings are almost as good as seeing the real thing—and a picture lasts much longer!

The monarch butterflies haven't come back from their vacation yet. Millions of them spend the winter months on the same twelve mountaintops in Central Mexico every year! José told me that the monarchs fly back to Texas every spring. He counts all the butterflies he sees around his yard and reports how many he finds on a monarch migration Web site. He says that this helps scientists track the monarchs each year. Walita and José are members of the Lepidopterists' Society (that's a fancy name for the national butterfly club), so they know a LOT about monarch butterflies!

Your budding lepidopterist,

Ashley

P.S. I want to raise butterflies!

On the second day of Christmas,
my cousin gave to me . . .

2 butterflies

and a mockingbird in a nut tree.

Dear Mom and Dad,

When we left on our road trip, Lito drove us right by the State Fair of Texas fairgrounds. Do you know which EXTREMELY tall Texan greets the visitors there? Big Tex—a very friendly-looking 52-foot cowboy statue! The Texas state motto is "Friendship," and the word "texas," or tejas, comes from a Native American word meaning "friends." Obviously Big Tex is the perfect symbol for this friendly state!

The farther east we drove, the more the land changed from flat plains to pretty green hills with groves of tall trees. (Some were huge pecan trees!) Before I knew it, we arrived in Tyler—the Rose Capital of the Nation—where we toured the Tyler Rose Museum. The Tyler Municipal Rose Garden is the nation's largest rose garden with nearly 40,000 rosebushes!

Tyler roses are famous all over the world. More than half of the nation's rosebushes come from this area, and every October they hold the Texas Rose Festival where they crown a Rose Queen. I bet everything smells like roses during that festival!

Fragrantly yours,
Ashley

P.S. Walita doesn't know we bought her a rosebush. It's hidden in the trunk!

On the third day of Christmas,
my cousin gave to me . . .

3 rosebuds

TYLER

2 butterflies,
and a mockingbird in a nut tree.

Dear Mom and Dad,

This trip just gets better and better! Today we drove through the largest city in Texas. The skyscrapers in downtown Houston were so tall and shiny, it looked like they were made of mirrors. Lito surprised us with a detour to NASA's Johnson Space Center where we watched a movie about space travel on an enormous, five-story screen. For a minute there, I thought we were really blasting off into space!

AND we made it to the Gulf of Mexico today! Lito and Walita took us to a restaurant on one of the piers where we ate fried shrimp as big as my hand! José says that during the summer you can sit outside and watch the shrimp boats return with their day's catch.

You won't believe this, but it was 75 degrees today! We spent the whole afternoon at the beach. I love how the air smells here—like salt and the sea. José and I combed the beach and found lots of interesting shells, including some lightning whelks. Walita told us that the lightning whelk is the state seashell and is named for its zigzaggy stripes. I can't wait to show you!

Your beachcomber,
Ashley

P.S. José gave me the sand dollar he found!

Dear Mom and Dad,

Did you know that the Texas state capitol building in Austin is made of pink granite and stands even taller than the United States Capitol? When I stood on the gigantic star in the middle of the floor and looked way up to the top, I got dizzy!

As we drove out of town, Walita cranked up the radio and we sang along with Willie Nelson's song, "On the Road Again." I'd never heard of him, but José says he's a really famous singer from Texas. Live music is so popular in Austin that they call it the "Live Music Capital of the World."

In this part of Texas, you can see why the prickly pear cactus was named the state plant. It grows EVERYWHERE—poking out of rocks, even growing upside-down from limestone cliffs. Almost every part of the prickly pear cactus is edible—except for the spines, of course! Locals eat the pads, or nopales, like a vegetable, and the fruit can even be made into candy.

During this trip, José and I have been counting pickup trucks on the highways. We stopped at a truck show so Lito could show us an old pickup like one he used to drive. A man there told us that Texas leads the nation in the sale of pickup trucks. I believe him!

On the road again . . .
Ashley

On the fifth day of Christmas, my cousin gave to me . . .

5 pickup trucks

4 lightning whelks, 3 rosebuds, 2 butterflies, and a mockingbird in a nut tree.

Dear Mom and Dad,

I finally got to see the Alamo! I learned that "Remember the Alamo!" was what Sam Houston's troops yelled at the Battle of San Jacinto, where "Texians" finally won their independence from Mexico.

Can you believe that Texas has been ruled by six different nations? Flags from Spain, France, Mexico, the Republic of Texas, the Confederate States of America, and the United States of America have all flown here. Since the state flag is red, white, and blue with a single star, it makes sense that we call Texas "the Lone Star State."

I ate so much today I had to take a _siesta_! For lunch we celebrated with Walita's favorite Tex-Mex Christmas tradition—_tamales_. We ate downtown on a dining boat while we floated on the San Antonio River! Then we went shopping at some of the stores along the river. This part of the river is called the _Paseo del Rio_, or the River Walk. And every April during Fiesta, decorated boats parade through town on the river. Someday I'd like to see that!

Remembering the <u>Alamo</u>,
Ashley

P.S. Walita told me that "alamo" is a Spanish word that means cottonwood tree.

On the sixth day of Christmas, my cousin gave to me . . .

6 flags a-flyin'

Remember the ALAMO!

5 pickup trucks, 4 lightning whelks, 3 rosebuds, 2 butterflies, and a mockingbird in a nut tree.

Dear Mom and Dad,

José and I are having the BEST time with Walita and Lito! This morning we went spelunking! (That's cave-exploring.) We walked down, down, down into the cool cavern (with a tour guide, don't worry) and saw stalactites, stalagmites, and a 100-foot waterfall inside!

Many caves around central Texas are home to millions of bats for nine months of the year. I wish the bats had been at home, but they spend their winters farther south—just like the monarch butterflies.

After lunch, we went fishing on the Guadalupe River. In the warmer months, Texans go "tubin'" here. They rent big inner tubes upriver and then float downriver, sometimes for miles! I HAVE to come back in the summer so I can try that!

Lito and I didn't catch as many fish as Walita and José, but we landed the largest. (Lito helped me reel it in.) Another name for the black bass we caught is the Guadalupe bass. José said that he's been fishing with Lito for years on this river and never knew that the bass they loved to catch was the state fish.

Swimmingly yours,
Ashley

P.S. My fish weighed 2 pounds!

On the seventh day of Christmas,
my cousin gave to me . . .

7 bass a-swimmin'

6 flags a-flyin', 5 pickup trucks, 4 lightning whelks,
3 rosebuds, 2 butterflies,
and a mockingbird in a nut tree.

Dear Mom and Dad,

On our way south, we talked Lito into stopping at the Texas State Aquarium in Corpus Christi. The sea turtle sanctuary was my favorite exhibit. Or maybe the otters were my favorite. I loved watching them play. They are so smart!

Lito said it was time to meet some real, live longhorns, so this afternoon we toured the King Ranch, the largest cattle ranch in the country. The name "longhorn" sure does fit these animals since some steers' horns span over six feet!

Our guide told us that way back in the 1800s, Richard King, a riverboat captain, started this huge longhorn ranch. The King Ranch now covers 825,000 acres and is bigger than the state of Rhode Island!

From 1867 to 1884, some of the ranch's longhorn cattle were driven by cowboys along the Chisholm Trail, which ran from the Rio Grande to central Kansas. Because of these cattle drives, the cowboy became a symbol for the West, and especially for Texas.

Whoopie-ti-yi-yo!
Ashley

P.S. José thinks he's a cowboy.

Dear Mom and Dad,

   We set up camp in Big Bend National Park today. The views are incredible! Until now, I didn't even know that Texas had mountains and canyons.

   José and I explored a flat, rocky area while Walita and Lito relaxed in the sun. And guess what else was relaxing on the warm rocks? A fat little horned lizard, which is the state reptile. He looked just like a miniature dinosaur! We were lucky to see him, since there aren't too many horned lizards in the park.

   Twenty-two species of lizards live in Big Bend National Park, including the Texas banded gecko. At dinnertime I met one up-close and personal. It leaped onto my arm, then ran across my sandwich! Ew!

   Tonight as I started writing this letter, I heard a strange snuffling sound next to me. When José and I peeked outside, we saw a large family of javelinas munching the prickly pear cactus right outside our tent! Javelinas look like wild, hairy pigs, but they're just cousins to the pig. Once they caught a whiff of us, they took off in a cloud of dust. (Lito says that javelinas can't see well, so they use their sense of smell to sense danger.)

   Wide awake now,
   Ashley

On the ninth day of Christmas,
my cousin gave to me . . .

9 leapin' lizards

8 grazin' longhorns, **7** bass a-swimmin',
6 flags a-flyin', **5** pickup trucks,
4 lightning whelks, **3** rosebuds, **2** butterflies,
and a mockingbird in a nut tree.

Dear Mom and Dad,

On our way to the Panhandle from Big Bend, José and I counted ten armadillos. Even though they look a little like reptiles with all those plates and scales, armadillos aren't related to lizards and snakes. They are mammals and distant cousins of the anteater. Lito told us that armadillos are good swimmers, but they sometimes cross a river by swallowing air so they can float across or they just walk on the river bottom UNDERWATER! They sure are funny little creatures.

Have you ever heard of a WIND farm? I hadn't until we passed by one today in West Texas. The turbine towers are GIGANTIC! Some are over 300 feet tall (that's as tall as a 30-story building). The blades on top look like huge white pinwheels. They twirl in the wind like old-time windmills and generate electricity. (And windy West Texas is the perfect spot for them!)

From Midland Walita drove north while Lito napped (gosh, he snores LOUD). Walita surprised us all with a trip to the Cadillac Ranch near Amarillo. Lito laughed and laughed. None of us had ever seen graffiti-covered Cadillacs, especially not nose-down in a field!

Your Cadillac kid,
Ashley

P.S. Lito said he's going to paint his Cadillac.
Walita doesn't think so.

On the tenth day of Christmas, my cousin gave to me . . .

10 armadillos

9 leapin' lizards, **8** grazin' longhorns,
7 bass a-swimmin', **6** flags a-flyin', **5** pickup trucks,
4 lightning whelks, **3** rosebuds, **2** butterflies,
and a mockingbird in a nut tree.

Dear Mom and Dad:

On our way back to the Metroplex (that's what Texans call the Dallas/Fort Worth area), we took a little detour to Glen Rose. We stopped at Dinosaur Valley where we got to see real fossilized dinosaur tracks. They were ENORMOUS!

A bunch of dinosaurs roamed Texas more than 100 million years ago. In 1908, a big flood caused the land to shift and buckle, and about a year later, a local teenager named Ernest Adams discovered dinosaur tracks in a branch of the Paluxy River. I wish that could've been me!

In 1938, a paleontologist named Roland T. Bird discovered more dinosaur footprints in that same area. Scientists now think that the carnivore Acrocanthosaurus atokensis made most of the tracks around Dinosaur Valley State Park and that it may have been the only giant carnivore of its time. It was slightly smaller than T. rex and lived in the Early Cretaceous Period (110 million years ago). That's about 45 million years before T. rex. I guess I got a little carried away with the dinosaur facts, but you know how much I LOVE dinosaurs! Maybe I'll be a paleontologist when I grow up!

Having a roaring good time,

Ashley

P.S. Walita helped me spell the really big words.

WELCOME TO
DINOSAUR
VALLEY
Glen Rose, TX

On the eleventh day of Christmas, my cousin gave to me . . .

11 dino fossils

10 armadillos, **9** leapin' lizards, **8** grazin' longhorns,
7 bass a-swimmin', **6** flags a-flyin', **5** pickup trucks,
4 lightning whelks, **3** rosebuds, **2** butterflies,
and a mockingbird in a nut tree.

Dear Mom and Dad,

You wouldn't believe all the incredible cowboy art we saw at the Amon Carter Museum in Fort Worth. My favorites were the bronze sculptures of Native Americans and cowboys by Frederic Remington and Charles Russell—artists who lived in the late 1800s and early 1900s. I could see every wrinkle and fold in those cowboys' clothes!

Then, we went to see a RODEO at the Fort Worth Stockyards. (Lito told us that the first rodeo in history took place in 1881 in Pecos, Texas.) Hooves, dirt, and hats flew! Eventually so did most of the cowboys when the broncos bucked off their riders. Only a few of the cowboys finished their 8-second rides. Walita told us that Lito used to ride in rodeos! I never knew that about my abuelo. José and I bought matching cowboy boots and pretended we were bronc' riders like Lito!

Later we danced at Billy Bob's Texas—the largest honky tonk in the world. ("Honky tonk" is another name for a dance hall.) Billy Bob's covers three acres and can hold more than 6,000 people. It even has its own indoor rodeo! You should've seen Lito and Walita. They waltzed and two-stepped all over that big dance floor.

Abrazos y besos,
Ashley

P.S. I can't wait to take another Texas road trip!

On the twelfth day of Christmas, my cousin gave to me . . .

12 buckin' broncos

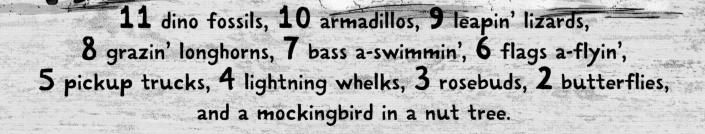

11 dino fossils, **10** armadillos, **9** leapin' lizards,
8 grazin' longhorns, **7** bass a-swimmin', **6** flags a-flyin',
5 pickup trucks, **4** lightning whelks, **3** rosebuds, **2** butterflies,
and a mockingbird in a nut tree.

¡Bienvenido a Tejas!

Texas: The Lone Star State

Capital: Austin • **State abbreviation:** TX • **Largest city:** Houston • **State bird:** the mockingbird • **State flower:** the bluebonnet • **State tree:** the pecan tree • **State insect:** the monarch butterfly • **State reptile:** the horned lizard • **State mammal (large):** the Texas longhorn • **State mammal (small):** the armadillo • **State flying mammal:** the Mexican free-tailed bat • **State seashell:** the lightning whelk • **State motto:** "Friendship"

Some Famous Texans:

Laura Lane Welch Bush (1946–) was born in Midland. A "bookworm" since childhood, she always loved to read, and was a second grade teacher and a librarian before she became First Lady of the United States. Laura established the National Book Festival in 2001 and continues to encourage children to read through numerous literacy programs.

Howard Robard Hughes, Jr. (1905–1976) was born in Houston, and first became famous for producing and directing controversial films. But this very eccentric industrialist, aviator, and self-taught engineer also greatly influenced aviation and the airline industry, becoming a billionaire in the process.

Barbara Charline Jordan (1936–1996) was born in Houston. She was the third African-American woman to practice law in Texas, and in 1967 became the first African-American woman to serve as a Texas state senator. Jordan was elected to the United States House of Representatives in 1972.

Sandra Day O'Connor (1930–), born in El Paso, was the first woman to serve as an Associate Supreme Court Justice of the United States. She was elected in 1981, and in her first year she received more letters from the public—60,000!—than any other Justice in history. She retired from the bench in 2006.

Quanah Parker (?–1911), last chief of the Quahadi Comanche tribe in Texas, was the son of a Comanche warrior, Noconie, and a white Texan woman, Cynthia Ann Parker. Parker was a resourceful leader who tried to protect his tribe's way of life.

Lee Buck Trevino (1939–) was born in Dallas. This famous professional golfer of Mexican descent taught himself to play golf at a very early age. As an adult, Trevino won numerous tournaments and in 2000 was ranked as the 14th-greatest golfer of all time.

To my dad—always a Texan,
who never considered being
anything else.

—J.B.

Spanish Glossary / Pronunciation

abrazos y besos	*ah-brah'-sos ee bay'-sos*	hugs and kisses
abuela	*ah-bway'-la*	grandmother
abuelo	*ah- bway'-lo*	grandfather
Bienvenido a Tejas	*bee-en-vay-nee'-doh ah tay'-hahs*	Welcome to Texas
boca	*bo'-kah*	mouth
cabaña	*cah-bah'-nya*	cabin
Feliz Navidad	*fay-lees' nah-ve-dahd'*	Merry Christmas
holá	*o-lah'*	hello
jalapeños	*hah-luh-peyn'-yohs*	a hot green or orange-red pepper used in Mexican cooking
javelina	*hah-vuh-lee'-nah*	wild, pig-like, hoofed mammal
Lito	*lee'-toh*	nickname for *abuelito*, "little grandfather"; from *abuelo*
nopales	*no-pahl'-es*	prickly pear pad
Señor	*seyn-yor'*	Mister
siesta	*see-es'-tuh*	afternoon nap or rest
tamales	*tah-mah'-les*	a Mexican dish made with spicy meat surrounded by cornmeal, wrapped in a cornhusk, then steamed
Walita	*wah-lee'-tuh*	nickname for *abuelita*, "little grandmother"; from *abuela*

STERLING and the distinctive Sterling logo are registered trademarks of Sterling Publishing Co., Inc.

Library of Congress Cataloging-in-Publication Data
Bynum, Janie.
The twelve days of Christmas in Texas / written and illustrated by Janie Bynum.
p. cm.
Summary: Ashley writes a letter home each of the twelve days she spends exploring the state of Texas at Christmastime, as her cousin José shows her everything from a mockingbird in a nut tree to twelve bucking broncos. Includes facts about Texas.
ISBN 978-1-4027-6350-2
1. Texas--Juvenile fiction. [1. Texas--Fiction. 2. Christmas--Fiction. 3. Cousins--Fiction. 4. Letters--Fiction.] I. Title.
PZ7.B9888Twe 2009
[E]--dc22

2008053403

2 4 6 8 10 9 7 5 3 1
6/09

Published by Sterling Publishing Co., Inc.
387 Park Avenue South, New York, NY 10016
Text and illustrations copyright © 2009 by Janie Bynum
The original illustrations for this book were created using traditional watercolor and digital media.
Designed by Kate Moll and Patrice Sheridan
Distributed in Canada by Sterling Publishing
c/o Canadian Manda Group, 165 Dufferin Street
Toronto, Ontario, Canada M6K 3H6
Distributed in the United Kingdom by GMC Distribution Services
Castle Place, 166 High Street, Lewes, East Sussex, England BN7 1XU
Distributed in Australia by Capricorn Link (Australia) Pty. Ltd.
P.O. Box 704, Windsor, NSW 2756, Australia

Printed in China
All rights reserved

Sterling ISBN 978-1-4027-6350-2

For information about custom editions, special sales, premium and corporate purchases, please contact Sterling Special Sales Department at 800-805-5489 or specialsales@sterlingpublishing.com.

Fiesta® is a registered trademark of The Fiesta® San Antonio Commission. All rights reserved.

Dr Pepper® is a registered trademark of Dr Pepper/Seven Up, Inc., All rights reserved.

Blue Bell Ice Cream® is a registered trademark of Blue Bell Creameries, Inc. All rights reserved.